CHESNEY
runs into Trouble!

Kes Gray & Mary McQuillan

Hodder Children's Books

A division of Hachette Children's Books

Hello! I'm Nurse Nibbles,

and these are my get well friends.

In my home, I have lots of hospital beds of ALL shapes and sizes.

Which is a good job because poorly animals
come to visit me from ALL over the world!

I've looked after ferrets with fractures,

tigers with toothache,

jellyfish with jaundice,

snails with sniffles,

and even llamas with laryngitis.

This morning a new poorly patient came to see me. His name was Chesney the cheetah and he looked very odd indeed.

This is the story of how Chesney the cheetah ran into trouble...

One day, Michael the meerkat was training Chesney the cheetah for the Champion of Champions Cheetah Championship Chase Race.

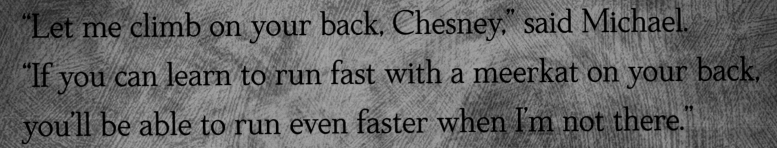

"Let me climb on your back, Chesney," said Michael. "If you can learn to run fast with a meerkat on your back, you'll be able to run even faster when I'm not there."

And Michael was right!

The next day, Michael arrived with a zebra.

"If you can learn to run fast with the two of us on your back, Chesney, you'll be able to run super fast when we're not there."

And Michael was right.

The following day,
Michael turned up
with the zebra and
a rhino!

"Chesney, if you can learn to run fast with all three of us on your back, you'll be able to run super-duper fast when we're not there."

And Michael was right again.

Every day, Michael trained Chesney
as well as he possibly could.

By the start of the race, Chesney was fitter and faster than he had ever been in his life.

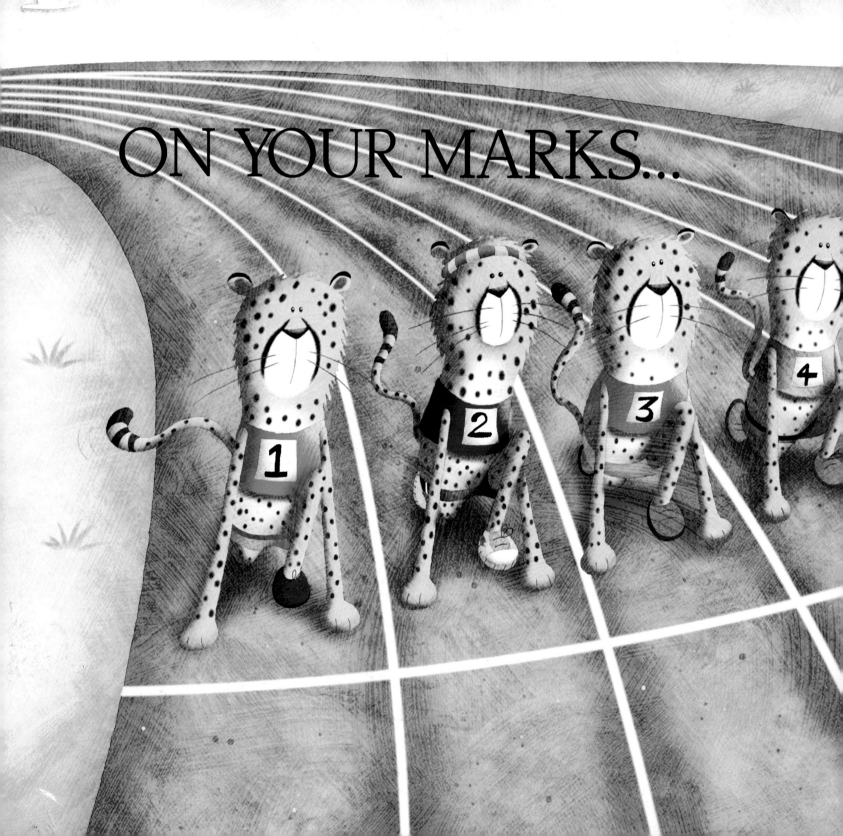

ON YOUR MARKS...

GET SET...

By the 'G' of 'GO!', Chesney
was halfway down the track!

By the 'O' of 'GO!', he had already crossed the line!

Chesney raised his paws
triumphantly as his
chest broke the ribbon.

He had won the Champion of Champions Cheetah Championship Chase Race in a super-duper-wuper fast time!

But there was one problem. His spots had fallen off along the way!

"Oh, dear!" said Michael. "You ran so fast, Chesney, your spots couldn't keep up!"

Oh dear indeed!

No wonder Chesney came to see me.

Never mind. The good news is that
Chesney won first prize for taking his
medicine, and was champion at putting
his feet up too.

He began to feel better in record time, and I'm pleased to report that Chesney the super-fast cheetah did get his spots back in...

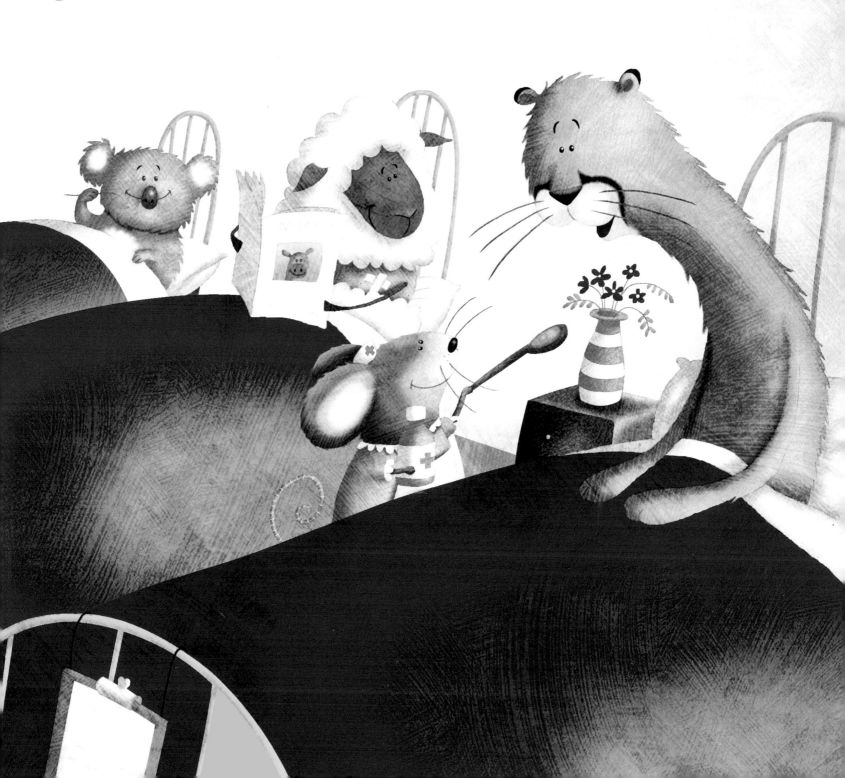

... THE END!

Emo the Elephant

Beyonce the Bear

Nurse Nibbles

Momo the Monkey

George the
Giant Snail

Giselle the Giraffe